吉高寧々

NENE YOSHITAKA
PHOTO BOOK

LOCATION IN RUSSIA OF KHABAROVSK

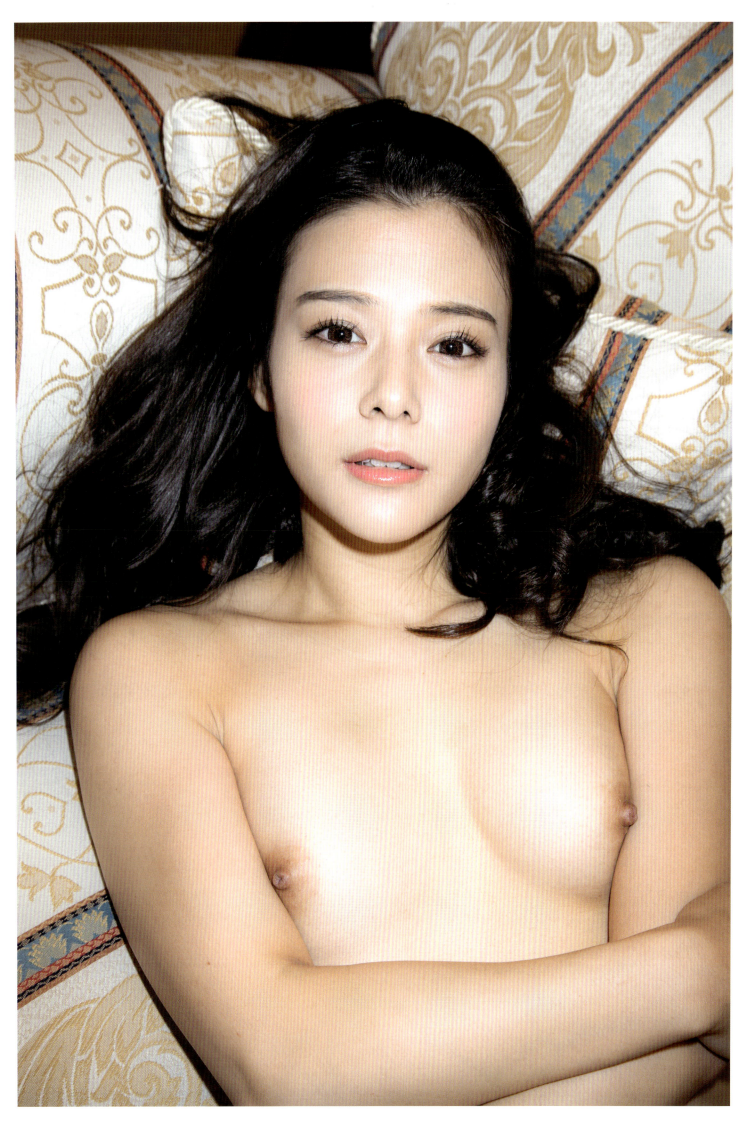

NENE YOSHITAKA
PHOTO BOOK
LOCATION IN
RUSSIA OF KHABAROVSK

Artist: NENE YOSHITAKA
Photographer: SUSUMU MAKIHARA
Assistant Photographer: RINTARO URYU
Styling: MAI OOKA & NENE YOSHITAKA
Hair and make-up: MAI OOKA
Artist Management: TADAHIKO GOTO (EIGHTMAN PRODUCTION)
Art Director: RYOTA MIZUKI
Editor: HIROSHI SHIBATA (TAKESHOBO)

本書の無断複写・複製・転載を禁じます。
定価はカバーに表記してあります。
©2018 Takeshobo Co.,Ltd.

※【特典チェキ】はカメラの性質上、写りが多少ボケていたりするのもありますがご了承ください。
また特典チェキに関する苦情・クレーム等に関しては受け付けておりませんので宜しくお願いします。